Dedicated to:

Paige Sophia & Kaitlin Elliot
Johnny & Gena & Andrew

Thank You to:

Birdie for divine inspiration
Pam Amodeo
Janine Drozd
Mary Ann Wheaton
&
Broadthink

zenda

The Crystal Planet

zenda

The Crystal Planet

created by
Ken Petti and John Amodeo

written with
Cassandra Westwood

Grosset & Dunlap • New York

Copyright © 2004 by Ken Petti & John Amodeo. All rights reserved. Published by Grosset & Dunlap, a division of Penguin Young Readers Group, 345 Hudson Street, New York, New York 10014. GROSSET & DUNLAP is a trademark of Penguin Group (USA) Inc. Printed in the U.S.A.

Library of Congress Cataloging-in-Publication Data is available.

ISBN 0-448-43255-2   10 9 8 7 6 5 4 3 2 1

Contents

Dreams Under the Stars *1*

Through Time and Space *11*

Crystallin *25*

Lies and Levitation *35*

Suddenly Free *51*

Connections *57*

The Palace of Gems *73*

The Cavern of Kelara *87*

Zenda's Vision *99*

Facing the Yowi *106*

One More Surprise *112*

Farewell to Crystallin *119*

A Moonlight Musing *125*

Last week, I thought I was the luckiest girl on Azureblue.

First, I escaped from this weird dimension where everyone thought I was great. I know that sounds like a good thing, but believe me, it wasn't.

I also found two more missing pieces of my gazing ball. Every girl and boy on the planet gets one when he or she turns twelve-and-a-half, but I dropped mine, and it broke into thirteen pieces. I've found three pieces so far, and I have to bind the other ten before I turn thirteen.

And the very best thing was when my mother and father told me we were going to visit my cousins on the planet Crystallin! I had never been off the planet before, and I couldn't wait to explore the universe. It was going to be the best vacation ever . . .

But nothing ever seems to go smoothly in my life. My cousins Stella and Kaitlyn are both really nice, but Stella can be a little, well . . . wild. I got swept up in Stella's glittering world on Crystallin, and almost got into big trouble—again.

You can read all about what happened to me on Crystallin. I know its one vacation I will definitely never forget!

Cosmically yours,
Zenda

Dreams Under the Stars

Zenda stepped out onto her front porch. She carried a small wicker basket in one hand. A tapestry of stars twinkled in the velvety blue sky above her. On the path ahead, bushes of white roses gave off a peaceful glow in the moonlight.

Normally, Zenda would have stopped to admire their beauty. But tonight she was too annoyed.

"The water lavender needs pruning before we leave," her father, Vetiver, had told her. "I thought you were going to prune the plants last night?"

"But I was packing," Zenda protested.

Vetiver looked around Zenda's room. Normally messy, tonight it looked like a whirlwind had hit it. Clothes were strewn over her bed, over her green velvet chair, and even all over the floor, covering the stacks of books that sprouted around her room like mushrooms.

"I see you got a lot accomplished," Vetiver said, smiling.

Zenda sighed. Her father wouldn't understand. She and her parents were traveling to the planet Crystallin to see Zenda's cousins. Zenda had no idea what girls her age wore on Crystallin, and she was only allowed one bag in the transport tunnel. She wanted to make sure she packed exactly the right clothes.

"Those plants need to be pruned," Vetiver said in that firm voice that meant Zenda should not even bother to argue with him. "You can pack when you are finished."

So Zenda was annoyed as she stepped off her porch, stopping to pluck a moonglow flower from the side of the house. The glowing flower lit the way as she headed down the path to the pond.

Most parents in Zenda's village would not have sent their twelve-year-old daughter out to prune plants at night, Zenda mused as she walked, but Zenda's parents were not most parents. Vetiver and Verbena owned Azureblue Karmaceuticals, the largest karmacy on the planet. They produced healing elixirs, aromatherapy oils, and other lotions and potions, all made from plants. Zenda had been helping with the business ever since she could walk.

So far, Zenda seemed destined to work with plants when she got older, too. At the age of thirteen, every child on Azureblue discovered that she or he had a special gift. But Zenda had shown signs of a gift when she was only twelve — *kani*, the gift of communicating with plants.

As she neared the pond, Zenda tried to quiet her annoyance. Plants could usually sense what mood she was in, and if the water lavender thought she was unhappy, the pruning wouldn't be easy.

Zenda found the small rowboat on the edge of the pond, climbed in, and pushed away from the pond's edge. The stalks of the water lavender grew on top of the water, and the roots extended underneath the surface. The plant had to be pruned at night, when the fragrant purple buds were closed. A much stronger oil could be extracted from the buds when they were closed.

The moonglow flower lit up a healthy clump of water lavender swaying gently on the water's surface. Zenda slowly rowed up next to it. Then she extended her hand and touched the plant.

Silently, Zenda asked the plant for permission to prune it. Then she waited for an answer.

It was difficult to describe how she heard the plants, Zenda always thought. It wasn't like she heard words, exactly. More like feelings.

After a few seconds, the plant's answer came to her—a sense of acceptance and happiness. Zenda stared at the plant in awe.

She still wasn't used to her gift, and sometimes she felt overwhelmed by the plants and how alive they were.

"Plants understand that we need to prune and harvest them," her mother, Verbena, always said. "They know they are part of the cycle here on Azureblue. They nourish us, and we nourish them."

Remembering Verbena's words, Zenda took a pair of sharp pruning scissors from the wicker basket and began to cut the stalks of lavender at the base. She made sure to leave plenty of stalks in the center of the plant. Soon, her basket was full.

"Thank you," Zenda said aloud. She looked at the full basket. Surely this would be enough to satisfy Vetiver. Zenda dipped the oar back into the black water.

Then she paused. All of the stars in the sky seemed to be reflected in the pond. She put the oar back in the boat and leaned over the side. It almost looked like she could scoop up a star, put it in her pocket, and carry it home.

Zenda searched the water to see if she could find Crystallin. Although it was a planet, Crystallin glowed brightly in the night sky. Zenda spotted the planet's reflection a few feet away and rowed toward it.

She dipped her hand in the pond, watching the water ripple over the planet's surface. She didn't have to capture Crystallin and put it in her pocket, she knew. Tomorrow, she'd be standing on the planet with her own two feet. She could finally see the Crystal Planet for herself.

Zenda leaned back up in the rowboat and stared at Crystallin in the sky. Her mind began to drift. Her grandmother, Delphina, had been to Crystallin many times. When she was alive, Delphina had told Zenda stories of buildings made of shimmering crystals and streets paved with colorful gems. It sounded like a magical place.

I hope I fit in, Zenda worried. She had never met her cousins before, but her Aunt Nina and Uncle Ciro sent a family picture every year. Kaitlyn, who was ten, looked a little bit like Zenda's own father. That made sense, since Vetiver and Uncle Ciro were brothers. Stella, her older cousin, was fourteen. In the pictures, her blonde hair looked almost silver. She had looked much older than fourteen in the last picture.

But that's not what worried Zenda, exactly. She knew that Stella had received her gazing ball at age twelve-and-a-half. It was a tradition carried out on Crystallin as well as Azureblue. The gazing ball contained thirteen musings—messages and advice that help you on life's journey.

Zenda, who was now twelve-and-a-half, had also received a gazing ball. But unlike Stella, Zenda had tried to see her gazing ball a day early, and in the process, had broken it. It had shattered into thirteen pieces, which had immediately vanished.

Zenda had found three pieces already, but she had learned that there was no easy way to find them. And if she didn't find all of the pieces before she turned thirteen, she might not find out what her special gift was going to be. Everyone thought it was going to be *kani*, of course, but Zenda secretly hoped it might be something else.

The fact that she broke her gazing ball embarrassed Zenda. She wondered what her cousins would think. Would they laugh at her? She had always dreamed of going to Crystallin, but she didn't want the whole gazing ball incident to ruin everything.

If only I knew what my cousins were like. Will they like me? Zenda thought, and then she caught herself and smiled. The last musing she had found was, "The best thing about the future is that it happens one day at a time." Wanting to know the future had almost gotten Zenda trapped in another dimension. She didn't get her musing until she had learned her lesson.

Zenda looked up at Crystallin and smiled.

"All right," she said. "I won't worry about the future on Crystallin. But it's okay to dream a little, isn't it?"

Somewhere on the pond, a bullfrog croaked in reply.

Through Time and Space

The next morning, Zenda scrambled to get her bag packed. She tried to pack a different dress for every day they would be away, but could not fit four dresses into the purple canvas sack.

Zenda frowned. She had to take the blue dress; it matched her eyes. And her mother always said the green dress complemented Zenda's long, red hair.

"Zenda, hurry!" Vetiver called up the stairs. "We're going to be late!"

Zenda frowned and dug through the bag. She saw Luna, her doll, staring back up at her.

For a split second, Zenda thought about leaving Luna behind, but quickly stopped the thought. She couldn't leave Luna on Azureblue while she traveled across the universe to another planet. Luna just wasn't any doll; she had been Delphina's doll when she was a girl, and Delphina had given Luna to Zenda when she was born. Somehow, having Luna made Zenda feel connected to the grandmother she had loved so much.

With a sigh, Zenda pulled her yellow dress out of the bag, squeezed the other clothes, and pulled the drawstring tightly. She'd just have to wear one dress twice, that was all.

"Zenda!" her mother called now, her high voice sounding impatient.

"Coming!" Zenda cried. She ran down the stairs and found her parents outside, sitting in the horse-drawn red wagon they used on the farm. The house and Azureblue Karmaceuticals were all part of a large expanse of land used for growing, harvesting, and processing plants for the company. The karmacy staff used the wagon to pick up plants from other suppliers around the village, and to deliver the karmacy's products to the center of the village, where they could be distributed around Azureblue.

Today, Niko, one of the karmacy staff,

13

had the reins to the two gray horses that pulled the wagon. He smiled at Zenda as she came running out of the house.

"You must be in a hurry," he said. "You forgot your flower crown!"

Zenda blushed. On Azureblue, it was customary for a girl her age to wear a crown of flowers on her head. Most girls felt undressed without one. Zenda, however, had found her flower crowns to be a problem ever since she got the gift of *kani*. The flowers responded to her mood, which meant they changed color or dried up—or worse. Still, Zenda knew she should wear one.

She quickly ran to the fence and picked several white daisies growing against the fence post. Then she threw her bag into the wagon and climbed in next to her mother and father.

"We're ready, Niko," Vetiver called out. Niko clicked his tongue, and the horses broke into a trot.

Zenda's fingers worked quickly as she

began to twist the daisies together to form a crown. But when the wagon reached the gate at the end of the property, Zenda felt a sudden pang of sadness. She looked back at the green house at the top of the hill.

"What's the matter, starshine?" Vetiver asked.

Zenda turned back to her parents. "I don't know. I guess I've never been far from home before. And now . . ."

"You'll love Crystallin," her mother said. "And we'll be back home in just a few days."

Zenda marveled at that. Crystallin was so far away—a tiny dot in the sky—and yet they would be there and back in just a few days. It seemed amazing.

She finished the crown and put it on her head.

"That's lovely," Verbena said. Her honey-colored eyes shone with love.

"Thanks," Zenda said. "It's not the best color for the dress, though." She looked down at her dress. The soft purple material floated down her waist and ended just above her ankles. She chose purple, her favorite color, hoping to make a good first impression.

"If I know you, those daisies won't stay white for long," Vetiver teased.

"Dad!" Zenda protested. She hated to be reminded of her problem with the flower crowns.

"Sorry, starshine," Vetiver said. "I couldn't resist."

Zenda sighed and studied her parents. Verbena wore a long, brown skirt and a short-sleeved, light brown top. Her long, brown hair, streaked with gray, hung down her back. Vetiver sat next to her, a head taller. He wore his gray hair in a neat ponytail. Wire glasses framed his hazel eyes. Zenda could make out faded green stains on his white button-down shirt—a result of working with plants every day. Both of her parents seemed calm and relaxed.

Zenda felt exactly the opposite. She nervously tugged on the small silk pouch she wore on a cord around her neck, in case she found any of the missing pieces of her gazing ball. She had no idea whether she would be able to find them all the way on another planet, but she wanted to be safe, just in case.

The wagon traveled to the center of the village, then got on another path heading toward the hills. The transport tunnels, Zenda knew, were located somewhere on the hillside. She had been there once, as a very young girl, to welcome Delphina back from one of her journeys.

Zenda felt she could barely keep still as the hills got closer and closer. Finally, the transport center came into view.

The path opened up to a circular field, bordered by the hills on the far end. In the center of the field sat a round, white building. Zenda could see a line of people entering through one side of the building, and another line leaving through another. Colorful wagons like the one they were traveling in circled the building.

Niko pulled the wagon to a stop as close as he could to the entrance. Even before the wheels had stopped turning, Zenda had climbed out of the wagon. Then she grabbed her bag.

"Hang on there, starshine," Vetiver said. "Don't go to Crystallin without us!"

When everyone had left the wagon, Niko waved good-bye and turned the horses around. Then Vetiver led them to the line of travelers waiting by the door.

"Won't be long now," he said.

Zenda's stomach flip-flopped. Now her excitement was turning to fear. She had never traveled in a transport tunnel before. She heard they could leave you feeling a little queasy. Maybe she shouldn't have eaten that sunflower muffin at breakfast . . .

A familiar voice interrupted her thoughts.

"Zenda!"

Zenda turned to see her friend Mykal standing there with his Great Aunt Tess. Mykal smiled shyly and brushed a strand of shaggy blond hair from his face. Great Aunt Tess ran up and captured Zenda with a hug. *Great Aunt Tess always smells of roses,* Zenda thought as she stepped back.

"We had to come and see you off," Great Aunt Tess said. She was a large woman who wore her blonde hair piled on top of her head. She wore a soft pink dress that reminded Zenda, once more, of roses—roses without thorns. There was nothing sharp about Mykal's aunt.

"It's pretty amazing that you're going to Crystallin," Mykal said.

"I know," Zenda said. "I'm a little nervous."

I can't believe Mykal came to say good-bye, Zenda was thinking. *That's so nice.* Then again, most things about Mykal were nice. Mykal and Zenda had been friends since they could remember. Mykal loved plants, and helped out at Azureblue Karmaceuticals. Since his parents died a year ago, he lived with Great Aunt Tess.

"We'll take good care of Oscar for you," Mykal said.

Zenda smiled, thinking of her little brown dog. "I know you will," she said. "Thanks!"

Then Verbena tapped her shoulder. "It's our turn, Zenda," she said. "Let's go!"

Great Aunt Tess buried Zenda in another hug. Mykal started to wave good-bye, then stopped. He took something out of his pants pocket.

"I almost forgot," he said. "You know that psychic who lives in the woods? She asked me to give you this."

Mykal handed Zenda a small, purple envelope with her name written on it. Zenda knew it could only be from one person — Persuaja, the powerful psychic who lived in the Hawthorn Grove. She and Zenda had been through a lot together in the last few weeks.

"Thanks, Mykal," Zenda said. She tucked the note into her bag.

Then Verbena grabbed her hand and led her inside the building. Vetiver was talking to a man dressed in white, holding a clipboard.

Zenda looked around the room. In front of her stretched a long wall with several doors. Each of the doors was marked with the names of the planets in the solar system, and some of the moons of Azureblue.

Zenda had studied the transport tunnels as part of her astronomy project at school. The tunnels connected the different planets, allowing fast travel without the boundaries of time or space. Crystallin scientists had

21

actually discovered how to use the tunnels, and had brought the technology to Azureblue. The clean, efficient method of transportation fit right in with the simplicity of Azurean society, and the tunnels were used quite frequently. They had to be monitored carefully to make sure two people weren't using a tunnel at the same time.

The man in white led them to a door marked "Crystallin."

"You'll travel one at a time," he said. "Only one bag allowed per traveler. Now, who will be first?"

Zenda looked hopefully at her parents. She was nervous, but she couldn't bear the thought of waiting another second.

"Go ahead," Verbena said. "You'll find Aunt Nina and Uncle Ciro waiting for you on the other side."

Zenda nodded. She gave her mother and father a hug. Then she faced the white door.

"All right, miss," said the man in white.

"Step inside, please."

Zenda opened the door and stepped inside. The door clicked shut behind her.

She seemed to be in a plain, white room. Then Zenda looked up, and realized there was no ceiling. In fact, there seemed to be nothing but empty space above her. Her stomach flip-flopped again.

Then, suddenly, the room went black.

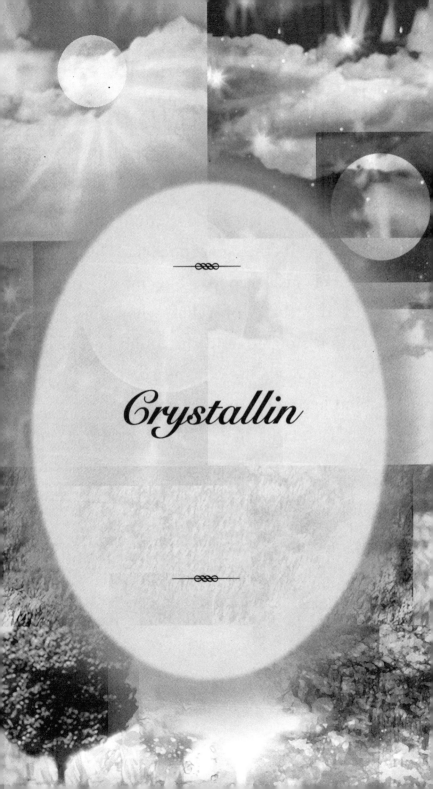

Crystallin

Suddenly, Zenda felt as though she was sliding through a liquid tunnel — not a watery liquid, but thick and fluid. Rainbow colors whirled past her face; she felt light-headed, yet strangely heavy at the same time.

Afterwards, Zenda could not quite remember if the sensation had lasted for hours, or just seconds. She mostly remembered the sense of relief when the liquid sensation stopped, and she found herself in a white room again. She heard a door open behind her and turned around.

"Zenda, is that you?" a booming voice asked.

Zenda stepped through the door, blinking from the bright light. A woman in a white uniform quickly swept past her and shut the door behind her.

The booming voice came from a tall, broad man with deep red hair, a bushy beard, and sparkling blue eyes that reminded Zenda of her grandmother Delphina.

"Uncle Ciro?" Zenda asked.

Zenda's uncle scooped her up and gave her a hug. "Look at you! It's a good thing you didn't end up looking like my big brother," he kidded.

Zenda realized he was talking about her father. Could this big man really be Vetiver's little brother? The idea seemed too strange.

"Goodness, Ciro. You'll crush her!"

A tall, thin woman stepped up and placed a hand on Ciro's shoulder. Her hair was a shade of blonde so pale it almost looked like moonlight. And her eyes—well, her eyes seemed to swirl with color, like the milky blues and pinks of an opal stone. Zenda knew from the pictures that this was her Aunt Nina.

"Hello," Zenda said shyly.

At that moment, there was the sound of a door opening, and Zenda's mother stepped through the transport tunnel into the room. Uncle Ciro scooped her up in his arms, too, and twirled her around.

Aunt Nina smiled and took Zenda's hand and led her toward the exit, where two girls sat on a white bench. Zenda recognized her cousins. Stella looked a lot like her mother, tall and thin. And in person, her silvery hair seemed to actually shimmer, as though it was made of spun diamonds. Kaitlyn was smaller than her mother and sister, with hazel eyes and light brown hair tied back in a ponytail.

Zenda heard the door of the transport tunnel again.

"That must be Vetiver," Aunt Nina said. "Girls, I want you to make your cousin feel at home." Then she turned and walked over to the other adults.

Zenda suddenly felt shy. Stella looked so exotic—just like she had expected a person from a far-off planet should look. What could she possibly have to say to someone like that?

But Kaitlyn, Zenda's younger cousin, spoke up first. "I love your flower crown, Zenda," Kaitlyn said, shyly standing up. "I've never seen so many different colors."

"Oh, no!" Zenda moaned. She took off her flower crown and saw that the white daisies had changed into a riot of rainbow hues. It had probably happened in the transport tunnel. "They're not supposed to be this way."

"I'm sorry," Kaitlyn said quickly. "I didn't mean—I just liked them, that's all."

Zenda felt sorry for her reaction. Kaitlyn seemed horrified at having upset Zenda. For a second, she reminded Zenda of a frightened field mouse she had stumbled on in the rose gardens once.

"Don't mind her," Stella said, shrugging. "Kaitlyn's always going on about plants and flowers. You'd think she lived on Azureblue or something."

Zenda felt her cheeks grow red. The way Stella said it, it didn't sound like she had such a high opinion of Azureblue.

Zenda handed the flower crown to

Kaitlyn. "Why don't you take it? I won't need to wear it here, since I'm not on Azureblue, anyway."

Kaitlyn looked shocked. "Th-th-thank you," she stammered.

Stella rolled her eyes. "Now you've done it," she said. "Kaitlyn will be following you around like a lost puppy. You'll never get rid of her now."

Is this teasing? Zenda wondered. Stella's attitude toward Kaitlyn seemed a little mean, but Zenda didn't have a sister—or a brother, for that matter—so she wasn't sure how sisters acted around each other.

At that moment, the parents joined them.

"Let's get out of here," Uncle Ciro said. "I'm sure Zenda wants to see Crystallin, not some waiting room."

Zenda eagerly followed along as Uncle Ciro led them outside the transport center. She stepped through the exit—and into the glittering world of Crystallin.

Zenda gasped. It was just as Delphina had described it. The path leading from the transport center was paved with cobblestones, but jewels in glimmering greens, reds, and blues had been added in with the stones. In the distance, Zenda could see the buildings of the city glittering in the sunlight. The effect was almost blinding.

Next to the transport building, Zenda noticed rows of low, white platforms, each about as big as their own red wagon. Uncle Ciro led them all to one of the platforms. It wasn't until Zenda got close to it that she realized it seemed to be floating inches off the ground. Curious, she bent down to examine it.

"What's holding it up?" she asked.

"Don't tell me you don't have zephyrs on Azureblue?" Stella asked.

"We don't need them on Azureblue," Vetiver said. "We have plenty of grass for horses there."

"That's right," Uncle Ciro said. "But we Crystallites had to find some other way to get around."

Aunt Nina, Stella, and Kaitlyn climbed onto the platform—the zephyr, Stella had called it. Uncle Ciro helped up Zenda's mother, and then lifted Zenda aboard as well. Then he and Vetiver climbed on. Zenda was shocked that the zephyr didn't sink at all underneath all of their weight.

Aunt Nina picked up a small, crystal square and began to move her finger over it in some kind of pattern. In the next instant, the zephyr began to move smoothly away from the transport building and floated down the road.

Zenda's parents chatted away with Uncle Ciro and Aunt Nina at the front of the pad. Zenda sat next to her cousins, not sure what to say. And really, there was so much to look at. As they got closer to the buildings, she saw that some were made of clear crystal, and others were made of smooth, polished stone.

Once again, it was Kaitlyn who broke the silence.

"Dad says you live on a big farm," she said. "With plants everywhere. A rose garden, and a greenhouse . . ."

Zenda nodded. "That's right," she said, but she didn't offer any more details. She hadn't come all the way to Crystallin to talk about plants! That's why she had been so excited to leave Azureblue in the first place.

"Tell me about where you live," Zenda asked Kaitlyn. "It must be so beautiful!"

"It is," Kaitlyn said. "Actually, last year Dad built me a greenhouse of my own. It's small, but I've been able to grow a lot there. I can't wait to show it to you!"

Kaitlyn looked so excited. Zenda held back a sigh. She couldn't disappoint her cousin, but looking at plants was the last thing she wanted to do on Crystallin.

Just then, Stella leaned over and

whispered in Zenda's ear. "Don't worry," she said. "I'll make sure you have a good time here. We're going to a party tonight—just don't tell Kaitlyn!"

*Lies and
Levitation*

Zenda could hardly believe it. She had only been on Crystallin a few minutes, and already she had been invited to a party by her teenage cousin. A small voice inside her wondered why Kaitlyn wasn't allowed to be told, but Zenda quickly dismissed it. Kaitlyn was only ten years old, after all. She probably wouldn't be interested in a teenaged party, anyway.

Moments later, the zephyr stopped in front of a house made of a creamy, pale pink stone. The low building, with its smooth walls and roof, looked so different from her two-story wooden house, with its creaky front porch and round cupola on the second floor.

Zenda jumped off the zephyr and followed her cousins inside. They stepped into a huge entryway with floors that looked like polished marble.

The entryway opened up into a huge room. White couches with cushions of silk circled a round, marble table that matched the floors. Next to one of the couches, a palm tree grew from a crystal tub.

Zenda's mother ran over to the tree in that quick way she had that made her always look like she was dancing. Verbena threw her arms around the skinny tree and hugged it. Zenda groaned inwardly. Her mother could be so embarrassing sometimes!

"Something green and alive!" Verbena said, taking a deep breath. "Crystallin is beautiful, but you don't have enough plants here at all."

"Ciro insists on keeping that in the gathering room," Aunt Nina said.

"I was born on Azureblue," Uncle Ciro said. "No one from Azureblue can be away from plants for too long. This little tree connects me to my roots."

Zenda had heard her grandmother tell Uncle Ciro's story many times. He had traveled to Crystallin with Delphina after finishing his schooling. It was supposed to be a short trip, but then he had met Nina—and had decided to stay on Crystallin forever.

It had broken Delphina's heart. "But," she had said, "love is stronger than time and space."

Zenda thought that was the most romantic thing she had ever heard. She looked at Aunt Nina, with her pale beauty, and understood why Uncle Ciro would want to stay. She tugged at her own red curls, which had become tangled in the transport tunnel, and wondered if anyone would ever feel that way about her.

"We'll have supper soon," Aunt Nina said. Zenda realized it was much later here on Crystallin than it had been when she left Azureblue. "I'll show Verbena and Vetiver to the guest room. Have you girls decided where Zenda will stay?"

Kaitlyn looked like she wanted to say something, but couldn't. Stella smiled sweetly.

"Zenda can stay with me," she said.

"Come on, Zen. I'll show you my room."

Stella tossed her shimmering hair and started to walk across the room toward an arched doorway. Kaitlyn ran up behind Zenda, bumping into her.

"Sorry," she said, blushing. "Maybe later, you can look at my greenhouse. Okay?"

"Sure," Zenda said.

And then she found herself gasping again.

They had entered a room with a huge pool of clear water in the center. Water trickled down the walls into the pool, making a musical sound.

"Is this your room?" Zenda asked Stella.

"Of course not," Stella said in a tone that made Zenda feel slightly embarrassed again. "Don't you have bathing rooms on Azureblue?"

"We have bathtubs," Zenda said. "But nothing like this. When we go swimming, we go to Crystal Creek."

Stella shook her head. "What a place. Sometimes I can't believe my own father came from there."

They passed through the bathing room and went down a staircase. It seemed to Zenda that they were traveling underground.

"All of our sleeping rooms are down here," Kaitlyn explained as though she had read Zenda's mind. "It's nice and dark and cool at night."

Stella pushed open the door of one room and turned to her sister. "That's nice, Kaitlyn," she said. "Now go leave us alone."

Zenda thought she saw a glimmer of fire in Kaitlyn's eyes, but it quickly vanished. Kaitlyn stomped off down the hallway, and Zenda followed Stella into her room.

Without windows, the room was very dark. But the walls seemed to be made of rock embedded with crystal, and large, luminous stones sat in each corner of the room, making the walls glow in the light. Stella had a huge bed with a puffy white bedspread, and a white rug on the floor that looked almost like it was made of feathers. Zenda put her canvas bag down on the floor and looked around.

"This is amazing," she breathed. "I've never seen anything like it!"

Stella shrugged. "It's not so bad. Lots of my friends have nicer rooms."

Opposite the bed, Stella had a huge dresser with shelves layered across the top like layers on a birthday cake. The cubbyholes in the shelves held shimmering stones in all colors. And one cubbyhole held a round, glass ball the size of an apple.

"Is that your gazing ball?" Zenda asked, and immediately wished she hadn't. The less she talked about gazing balls here, the better.

Stella walked up to the dresser and picked up the ball. "It sure is," she said. "It's nothing special, really. Is this what yours looks like? You got yours this year, didn't you?"

"Well, kind of . . ." Zenda said, her voice

trailing off.

Stella suddenly smiled. "Oh, right! I heard Mom and Dad talking about that. You broke yours, didn't you?"

Zenda could feel her face reddening. "It was an accident."

"You are so lucky," Stella said. "Gazing ball training was such a pain. All those musings! Like a year full of lectures." She sank down onto her big bed and twirled the gazing ball in her fingers.

Zenda relaxed. Stella obviously didn't care that she had broken her gazing ball. Now she felt more comfortable asking about Stella's ball.

"You turned thirteen last year, didn't you?" Zenda asked. "What gift did you get?"

Stella sat up. "I'll show you," she said.

Stella held her gazing ball in her palm. Nothing happened for a few seconds. Then, slowly, the gazing ball rose into the air.

"Wow," Zenda breathed.

Stella focused her eyes on the ball, and it began to move, making circles and loops in midair. Then she closed her eyes, and the ball dropped into her hand.

"Levitation," Stella said matter-of-factly. "I can't do big things yet. Just small things."

"That's totally amazing," Zenda said.

"I guess," Stella said. "It's not very useful. I mean, some of the rescuers use it to save people when mines cave in and stuff. You know, moving big rocks out of the way. But that's so boring! I don't want to do that for the rest of my life."

Before Zenda could reply, there was a knock on the door.

"Go away!" Stella yelled. But the door opened anyway, and Kaitlyn came in. She carried a crown made of pale green sage leaves.

"I wanted to thank you for the flower crown, Zenda," she said. "I grow sage in my greenhouse. It's not as pretty as a flower crown, but I thought you might like it."

Zenda took the crown, and the musty smell of sage filled her nostrils. It reminded her of home.

"Thanks, Kaitlyn," she said. She placed the crown on her head. Nobody on Azureblue wore herb crowns, but she wasn't on Azureblue. And she could always take it off for the party.

Stella laughed. "Nice weeds, Kait," she said. "But I've got something better for Zenda."

Stella raised her left hand, and the sage crown floated off Zenda's head and landed on the floor.

"Hey!" Kaitlyn protested, running over to pick it up.

Then Stella pointed a hand at her dresser. A glittering circle of stones floated off a shelf and landed on Zenda's head.

"That's more like it," Stella said.

Kaitlyn's eyes were wet with tears. She left the room and slammed the door behind

44

her without saying anything.

Zenda felt awkward, but when she caught a glimpse of herself in the dresser mirror, she had to admit that the crystal crown was truly lovely.

"Thanks, Stella," she said. "It's beautiful."

"No problem," Stella said. "Now let's go eat!"

Uncle Ciro had cooked a huge plate of cellophane noodles and star fruit.

"The tomatoes are canned," he said apologetically. "It's harder to get fresh veggies here than it is on Azureblue."

Still, Zenda thought the pasta was delicious. For dessert, Aunt Nina had made fruit flavored snowflakes.

Before they left the table, Stella turned to her mother. "I'm going to take Zenda to Ruby's Cafe tonight to meet Trisha and Celeste. Is that okay?"

Zenda was confused to hear Stella

mention the cafe. Hadn't she said something about a party? But Zenda didn't say anything.

"Of course," Aunt Nina said. "That is, if it's all right with Verbena and Vetiver."

"What kind of place is it?" Vetiver asked.

"The young kids like to hang out there," Uncle Ciro said. "Harmless fun."

"What about me?" Kaitlyn asked.

"Ruby's Cafe is for older girls, Kaitlyn," Aunt Nina said. "You know that."

Kaitlyn frowned and stared at her plate.

Verbena turned to Zenda and smiled. "Just don't stay out too late, sweetie."

Back in Stella's room, Zenda watched as Stella put shimmering blue powder over her eyes.

"The cafe sounds fun," Zenda said, not wanting to ask directly about the party.

"Oh, we're not going there," Stella said casually. "We're going to the party, remember? I just said that to throw off the boulders."

"Boulders?" Zenda asked, confused.

"You know," Stella said, applying silver powder to her cheeks. "Boulders. Adults. Big, boring rocks that never go anywhere or have any fun."

Zenda frowned. They didn't have a slang word like that for adults on Azureblue. And lying to the parents made Zenda uncomfortable. She had done that before herself—and it hadn't turned out very well at all.

Still, Stella seemed so confident. And Zenda didn't want to seem like . . . well, like a boring rock that didn't want to go anywhere or have any fun.

The night air was cool when they stepped outside. Above, Zenda was startled to see only one moon, rather small, shining in the night sky. Azureblue had four moons, and it was almost always possible to see two at once.

"Are we taking the zephyr?" Zenda asked.

"Nope," Stella said. "We're walking."

She reached into the silver silk pouch attached to her waist and pulled out two glowing rocks. She handed one to Zenda.

"It's not far," she said.

They walked past the houses, then turned onto a path that seemed to lead into the darkness.

"Are you sure this is a good idea?" Zenda asked a little nervously.

"Trust me," Stella said.

After a while, Zenda realized they were heading toward the hillside. They came to a steep slope, and Zenda almost stumbled on the way down. At the bottom, she saw a hole carved into the hill.

A loud beat, like a thumping heart, seemed to pulsate from inside the hill. Zenda wondered for a second if they were about to encounter some huge beast. But she didn't say anything, and followed Stella inside.

The hole opened into a huge, wide cavern that was larger than Zenda's village square. Crowds of teenagers were dancing to the beat of a strange kind of music. Lights in red, purple, and green pulsated from the cavern and seemed to be located everywhere, in every direction.

Stella turned to Zenda and smiled. "Still think this is a bad idea?"

Zenda smiled back. "Are you kidding? Let's dance!"

Suddenly Free

Stella grabbed Zenda's hand and led her down a long, twisting path to the bottom of the cavern. The music was much louder here. They pushed their way through the dancing crowd until they came to two girls.

Both girls looked like they were Stella's age, and they were similar in other ways, too. They were both tall, with blonde hair, although neither of them had shimmering hair, like Stella's. One girl wore her hair in four thick braids that swung as she danced. The other girl's hair was short and spiky. They both stopped dancing when they spotted Stella and Zenda.

"This is my cousin, Zenda," Stella said, nearly shouting so her voice could be heard over the music. "She's from Azureblue."

"That explains the dress," said the girl with the braids.

Zenda suddenly felt self-conscious. She had kept on her purple dress. It was one of her favorites, and she always thought she looked nice in it.

But she knew it didn't look anything like the outfits that Stella and her friends wore. They all wore short skirts, sleeveless tops, and boots. They looked like they had been woven of silk or maybe even spun crystal, and the material shimmered under the blinking lights. Zenda's dress was soft, faded cotton, and the bottom grazed the tops of her ankles.

"Don't be rude, Trisha," the spiky-haired girl said. "I think she looks cute. Kind of retro."

Trisha smiled sweetly. "Of course. Like something out of a storybook!"

Zenda felt a little better. Trisha's remark sounded kind of impolite—but it was nothing like what she got from Alexandra White, a girl in her school back home.

"This is Trisha and Celeste," Stella said.

"Nice to meet you!" Zenda shouted over the music.

But the girls didn't reply. They started

dancing again. Stella joined them, waving her arms in the air.

Zenda was relieved. She had no idea what to say to these girls. But dancing—that was easy. She closed her eyes and concentrated on the beat of the music. Then she began to twirl around on the dance floor.

Zenda couldn't help thinking about her mother. Verbena loved to dance, and had almost trained to be a dancer until she decided to devote her life to plants. She would probably love it here.

With a pang, Zenda realized she wouldn't be able to tell Verbena about it, thanks to that lie Stella had told about the cafe.

Zenda decided to think about something else. As she twirled, she studied the dancers at the party. Most of them looked like they were Stella's age, or maybe a little older. And many of them seemed to have blond hair, even the boys.

Of course, their hair was pale blond.

Not like Mykal's. His was golden, like the color of wheat just before it was cut down . . .

Zenda wasn't watching where she was going. Her stomach lurched as she tripped over the foot of another dancer. She held out her arms just in time, cushioning her fall.

A boy with black hair held out an arm to help her up. Before she could thank him, he turned back to his dance partner.

Zenda's face flushed. She was sure Stella would never take her anywhere again.

But Stella and her friends had their eyes closed, and hadn't even noticed her fall. Relieved, Zenda reached up to check her flower crown, on instinct. Back home, a fall like that would have resulted in her flowers turning bright red, or losing their petals or something.

But she wasn't wearing a flower crown, she remembered. There were crystals on her head, not flowers. In fact, there wasn't a single plant in the room. No flower garlands. No

55

potted trees. No sprawling arrangements of grasses and greens.

Zenda found herself smiling. Being far away from home, from her past, from the plants that bloomed and died and changed color around her, felt suddenly free. She spread her arms and began to twirl wildly.

Suddenly, a piercing, beeping sound filled the caverns. All of the dancers stopped at once. Stella ran over and grabbed Zenda's arm.

"Come on, Zen," she said. "Party's over."

Connections

Stella moved quickly. Zenda noticed that some of the kids stood, stunned, as if they didn't know what to do. But Stella pushed right past them, pulling Zenda along with her.

"What's going on?" Zenda shouted over the noise.

"I'll explain later," Stella said. "Just move."

They scrambled up the pathway and back to the cavern entrance. When they emerged, Zenda was blinded by an unexpected wave of bright light. Men and women wearing blue uniforms and carrying gas lanterns were hurrying toward the cavern. One of the women grabbed a boy with blond hair as he tried to run past.

Zenda felt terrified, but Stella seemed cool and calm. She kept running, weaving through the crowd, until they reached the main road.

Then she slowed down.

Zenda's heart was beating wildly. They seemed to have escaped whatever trouble was going on back at the caverns. But what had happened back there?

Stella led Zenda down another street to a stone building painted red. A sign above the door, illuminated by a row of glowing rocks, announced that it was Ruby's Cafe. Stella opened the door, led Zenda to a small table, and then sank down into her seat.

"That was close," Stella said.

Zenda sat across from her and rested her hands on the table. She saw that they were trembling.

"So, I guess that party wasn't supposed to happen, was it?" Zenda asked.

"Keep your voice down," Stella said, leaning across the table. "It's no big deal. We have parties in there all the time. But some people don't want us in the caverns. There are rare minerals down there, and they're afraid we're going to affect the ecological balance, or something. It's ridiculous. We're just having fun."

"What about those kids who got caught?" Zenda asked, thinking how easily it could have been them.

"They're fine," she said. "They get taken to their parents. Things will quiet down for a while, and then there'll be another party, in another cavern. That's how it goes."

The door swung open, and Zenda was startled to see her father and Uncle Ciro walk through the door.

"Heard there was a raid on one of the caverns," Uncle Ciro said, eyeing Stella carefully. "I just wanted to make sure you two were safe and sound."

"Of course," Stella said, smiling sweetly. "Zenda and I have been here all night, haven't we, Zenda?"

Zenda avoided her father's eyes. "Sure," she said.

"That's good," Uncle Ciro said. "Because I would hate to think that a daughter of mine would put her cousin in danger. That would be a really stupid thing to do."

Stella yawned. "I'm so tired. If you're done lecturing now, we'd like go to home."

Zenda stood up. Vetiver scanned her intently through his glasses, but seemed satisfied that everything was all right.

When they got back to the house, Zenda was relieved to see that someone had set up a pallet of comfortable cushions for her on the floor of Stella's room. Aunt Nina showed her a basket by the door of the room covered with a dark cloth. Inside were several of the small, glowing stones like the one Stella had given her earlier.

"Just take out one of those if you need to get up during the night," Aunt Nina said, then kissed her on her cheek.

After saying good-night to everyone and washing up, Zenda put on her white cotton nightgown and gratefully tumbled into bed.

"Night, Zen," Stella said, climbing into her fluffy white bed. "Hope you had fun."

"Thanks," Zenda said.

As tired as she was, Zenda found she couldn't sleep right away. She quietly slipped out of bed and retrieved her journal from her canvas bag. She removed one of the small rocks from the basket and climbed back under the covers. There was just enough light to write.

———❦———

Stella asked me if I had fun tonight. I guess I did. I mean, Crystallin is so beautiful. Everything sparkles and shimmers. And that party in the cavern was not like anything I've ever seen on Azureblue.

The last big party I went to was Camille's birthday party. We all went into the village for ice cream. Not as glamorous as the party tonight—but I don't know. I think maybe I had more fun with Camille.

It definitely wasn't fun when those alarms went off and we had to run out. I still can't believe we didn't get caught! Stella was smart to know to go to the cafe, too. She must have known Ciro would be looking for her. I don't think I would have thought of that. If this happened to me back on Azureblue, I definitely would have been caught. Vetiver would have made me weed the thorn bushes for at least two weeks.

But we didn't get caught. And I had fun dancing. Nobody made fun of the way I sometimes can't control my kani. Nobody even knows me here. I kind of like that feeling. It's like I can be anyone I want.

I'm glad Stella likes me. I wonder what we'll do tomorrow? I hope it's exciting—but not in exactly the same way tonight was exciting!

Cosmically yours,
Zenda

⊱⊰

Zenda closed the journal. She quietly walked across the room to return the rock to its basket. On the way there, she took one more thing out of her bag—Luna.

Minutes later, Zenda was fast asleep, with Luna tucked into her arms. Almost immediately, it seemed, she began to dream. She was standing on top of a glittering mountain, wearing a dress made of white spun silk. Rubies, emeralds, and sapphires danced above her head. Zenda waved her fingers like the conductor of an orchestra, making the stones move at will.

When she woke up, she found two midnight blue eyes staring right into hers. Zenda jumped. Kaitlyn was sitting on the floor, cross-legged, watching her.

"Mom said to wake you and Stella for breakfast," Kaitlyn whispered. "But you both looked so peaceful."

"Thanks," Zenda said, yawning. "I'm awake."

Kaitlyn pointed to Luna. "What's that?" she asked.

Zenda felt embarrassed. Most girls her

age had given up dolls by now. But Kaitlyn looked curious. She handed Luna to Kaitlyn.

"Her name is Luna," Zenda said. "Delphina gave her to me."

Kaitlyn gently touched Luna's face. "Granny Delphie told me about Luna," Kaitlyn said. "She's just like I imagined. You're so lucky to have her!"

For the first time, it dawned on Zenda that Delphina had been Stella and Kaitlyn's grandmother, too. Delphina traveled to Crystallin at least once a year—but Zenda had Delphina close to her most of the time. Kaitlyn was right—Zenda did feel lucky.

"Why don't you show me your greenhouse this morning?" Zenda suggested. She suddenly felt like doing something nice for Kaitlyn. Seeing a few plants wouldn't be the worst thing in the world.

"Really?" Kaitlyn squealed.

Stella stirred in her bed. "What? Who's that?" she asked sleepily.

"Thank you, Zenda," Kaitlyn said, throwing her arms around her. "I'll show you after breakfast."

Zenda dressed in her light blue dress and put the crystal crown on her head. Breakfast was cooked oatmeal and peaches—not fresh peaches, like Zenda was used to, but preserved peaches in a sweet syrup.

Stella slept through breakfast, and Zenda was grateful, because the subject of the night before did not come up at all.

"Stella can't stay in bed much longer," Aunt Nina said, smiling. "We're all going to the Gemology Museum this afternoon."

"But first Zenda's going to see my greenhouse!" Kaitlyn said eagerly.

Zenda pushed away from the table. "Let's go now," she said. She turned to her aunt and uncle. "Thanks for breakfast!"

Kaitlyn led Zenda to the back door of the house, which led to a gray stone patio. A small house made of glass had been built in the southern corner. Kaitlyn took a key she wore from a chain around her neck and unlocked the door.

Though the room was small, almost every inch was home to some kind of plant. Zenda noticed curiously that the plants were not potted in dirt. Many of them seemed to be growing out of long troughs of water.

"We don't have a lot of dirt here on Crystallin," Kaitlyn said, as though she was reading Zenda's thoughts again. "Mostly rocks. Most of the farmers in the south build greenhouses like this one. They grow the plants in water and add nutrients to feed the plants. It doesn't work with all plants, but some of them do really well."

Zenda was impressed. She recognized ten different kinds of herbs, and saw rows of cucumber plants growing, their healthy green leaves shooting upward.

"The cucumbers are for Dad," Kaitlyn said. "He loves them."

"You should be really proud, Kaitlyn," Zenda said. "If I didn't know better, I'd think you were from Azureblue."

Kaitlyn blushed, pleased. "Thanks," she said. "It's not much, though."

Zenda shook her head. "This is great. My friend Mykal would love this place. I bet he'd have lots of ideas for you."

"Does Mykal have the gift of *kani*, like you?" Kaitlyn asked eagerly.

"Mykal's not thirteen yet," Zenda explained. "And my *kani*—well, it came early. I'm not even sure if it's the real thing yet. I might get another gift when I turn thirteen. Maybe levitation, like Stella. That's pretty amazing."

Kaitlyn frowned. "I guess. I'd rather have *kani*. That's what I'm hoping for, anyway. But not many people on Crystallin get it."

Zenda was about to say something when a rosemary plant caught her eye. Its spiky leaves were turning dark brown, and many had fallen off.

Zenda frowned. She hated to see a plant that wasn't doing well. She walked over to it.

"Poor thing," Zenda said, gently touching the stalks.

The plant immediately responded to Zenda's touch. The drooping stalks began to stand up straighter. Then a feeling entered Zenda's mind—a feeling coming from the rosemary.

"It's too cold," Zenda said. "It needs more sunlight. You should move it closer to the glass."

Kaitlyn looked excited. "That was your *kani*, wasn't it?" she asked.

Zenda shrugged shyly. "I guess I'm controlling it a little better now. I used to make lots of mistakes with it."

Zenda started to tell Kaitlyn about some of the things that had gone wrong with her *kani*—like how she had caused a firebrush plant to explode into sparks in front of the village elders. The girls were laughing when Stella entered the greenhouse.

"Stop bugging Zenda with your boring plants, Kait," she said. "Mom says it's time to go."

The Palace
of Gems

A few minutes later, they all piled onto the zephyr, which Uncle Ciro steered down the road. In the distance, Zenda could see clusters of sparkling buildings sprouting from a low, flat hill.

"That is Thalissa, the cultural center of Crystallin," Aunt Nina explained as the zephyr moved swiftly and silently toward their destination. "It houses the meeting place of the elders, several art museums, the theater, the library, and the Palace of Gems."

"Dad works in the Museum of Sculpture," Kaitlyn said proudly.

Zenda realized that she had not even had an idea of what her Uncle Ciro did for a living. She had just assumed it had something to do with rocks.

Her uncle overheard Kaitlyn. He turned his head to smile at the girls. "You know how much Delphina loved art. She must have passed some of that down to me."

Delphina had not just loved art, Zenda

knew, but she created it as well. When she had turned thirteen, so long ago, Zenda's grandmother had been given a gift that allowed her to express emotions through her paintings. Looking at one of Delphina's creations could make you feel intensely happy or sad or even both things at once.

Stella suddenly got a wistful look on her face. "Delphina let me watch her paint once," she said. "It was really amazing. It was like she became part of the painting, almost. You know?"

Zenda nodded. "I saw her paint a few times. I know what you mean."

Soon, the zephyr reached the outskirts of Thalissa. Uncle Ciro pulled the zephyr into a low building that seemed to be a kind of zephyr storage area. They left the zephyr hovering inside the building and then stepped out into the center of Thalissa.

Zenda had never seen anything like it. Her cousins' house had been beautiful, but the buildings in Thalissa were larger, grander, and even more detailed with jewels and crystals. The largest building in Thalissa was a dome-shaped structure that rose above all the other buildings. What must have been millions of rubies, emeralds, and sapphires glittered across the top of the dome.

"That's the Palace of Gems," Aunt Nina said, noticing her expression. "We'll go there first."

"How exciting," Stella said loudly, in a voice that meant she clearly thought the Palace of Gems was the most boring place in the world.

"Come on now, Stella," Uncle Ciro said. "Your cousin has never seen the palace before. It's a real treat."

Stella sighed. "Yes, Dad," she sighed. But after the adults turned away and began to walk on ahead, Stella whispered in Zenda's ear.

"Don't worry," she said. "I'll get you out of this."

Zenda didn't like how that sounded. Stella had used the same tone when she talked about going to the party—and that hadn't turned out well at all. She wondered what Stella had in mind.

But her worries vanished as soon as they approached the Palace of Gems. Wide, marble steps led up to the arched entrance of the building. Zenda could only imagine what kinds of things waited inside.

Verbena walked up to her and squeezed her hand. "I was here once before, years ago," she said. "It's beautiful. Almost as beautiful as a rose garden in full bloom."

"But not quite, right?" Zenda asked. She knew that nothing could compare to her mother's love of plants.

"No," Verbena said, smiling. "Not quite."

They stepped inside the entrance. The room seemed to glow with soft, rainbow colors. Zenda realized the glow was coming from the different rocks and gems displayed around the room on white marble pillars.

"The palace holds a sample of every rock and mineral found on Crystallin," Uncle Ciro said. "There are thousands."

"And we'll probably look at every single one of them," Stella muttered under her breath.

Kaitlyn took Zenda's hand. "Come on," she said. "I'll show you my favorite."

Kaitlyn dragged Zenda across the room. Looking up, Zenda saw that there were several floors above them, circling the inside of the dome. Each floor held more pillars topped with more stones.

Kaitlyn stopped in front of a pillar with a white, milky stone. She walked up close.

"You have to look inside," she said.

Zenda did, and to her surprise, saw images inside the stone. A little girl with black hair was building a pyramid out of small rocks.

"It's a memory stone," Kaitlyn said. "It holds the memories of the person who owned it. This one was owned by one of the elders. They're very rare."

"That's amazing," Zenda said, shaking her head. The stone reminded her of Persuaja. One of the psychic's tools was a crystal pyramid. Persuaja could look inside the pyramid to see images of the past, present, and future.

Suddenly, Zenda remembered the purple envelope Mykal had slipped to her back at the transport tunnels. Persuaja had sent it, and she still hadn't opened it! She'd have to remember to do that as soon as she got back to the house.

Kaitlyn took Zenda from one stone to another. Stella walked slowly behind them, yawning every few minutes. But Zenda was too absorbed in the stones to worry about Stella. She saw a red stone that somehow burned with fire in the center; a blue stone that contained twinkling lights that looked like stars; and a yellow stone that contained a nutritious liquid when you cracked it open.

"It's all so incredible," Zenda breathed, and then she felt Uncle Ciro's hand on her shoulder.

"We're all going up to the second floor," he said. "Have you finished down here?"

"Actually, Zenda's not feeling too well," Stella said quickly. "I think I should rent a zephyr and send her home."

Uncle Ciro looked concerned. "Are you all right, Zenda?"

Verbena, Vetiver, and Aunt Nina joined them now. Zenda wasn't sure what to say.

Stella jumped in again. "I think it was those canned peaches," she said. "Right, Zenda?"

Zenda hesitated. She didn't want to lie, but she didn't want to disappoint Stella, either, for some reason. Stella already thought she was just a boring girl from backwards Azureblue.

"Right," Zenda said softly.

"Poor dear," Verbena said, feeling her forehead. "I'll go home with you."

"Oh, no, Aunt V.," Stella said sweetly. "I've seen the palace loads of times. I can take Zenda home."

Verbena and Vetiver exchanged worried glances.

"Stella always babysits Kaitlyn," Aunt Nina pointed out. "She's very responsible."

Zenda blushed. She didn't need a babysitter! But the idea seemed to satisfy Zenda's parents. Uncle Ciro gave Stella some coins to rent a zephyr, and they left the palace. Zenda could feel Kaitlyn's eyes on her the whole time.

"Don't worry about Kaitlyn," Stella said as they walked down the marble steps. "She won't tell. She never does."

"What are we going to do?" Zenda asked nervously.

Stella grinned. "The best thing in

Thalissa is not the Palace of Gems. It's the shopping! Come on."

Zenda followed Stella as she zigzagged through the crowded streets. Finally, they came to a stone shop embedded with rainbow-colored marbles. They stepped inside, and Zenda saw Trisha and Celeste looking at racks of clothes.

"About time," Trisha said.

"Tell me about it," Stella said. "So have you found anything?"

Celeste held up a short dress made of a shimmering, emerald-green material. "What about this one?" she asked. She held the dress up against Zenda.

"Oh, I can't go shopping," Zenda said. "I mean, I didn't bring any coins with me."

Stella fished out the coins Uncle Ciro had given her for the zephyr.

"No problem, Zen," she said. "We're covered. And now you're going to get a Crystallin makeover."

Before Zenda could protest, the girls pushed Zenda into the dressing room and started passing her outfit after outfit. Zenda felt uncomfortable at first, but soon discovered it felt nice to be the center of attention. And the clothes were beautiful.

After trying on just about every outfit in the store, Zenda came out in the green dress that Celeste first held up.

"Perfect!" Stella said.

"I could have told you that," Celeste teased.

Stella picked up Zenda's crumpled blue dress and dropped it into the shopping bag. Then she paid for the green dress at the counter.

Outside the shop hovered a small zephyr. Celeste climbed aboard, and the other girls followed.

"We'd better get you home before the boulders get there," she said, smiling.

As the zephyr floated out of Thalissa, Trisha braided Zenda's hair into long braids, then carefully wrapped them in a coil on top of Zenda's head. She wound the crown of crystals around the coil. Then Stella added sparkling green powder to her eyes.

"I have butterfly slippers you can borrow at home," she said. "You look like one of us now, Zen."

"No one would even guess you were from Azureblue," Trisha said, looking pleased.

I wonder what everyone back home would think, Zenda mused. *Clumsy Zenda, a sophisticated teenager from Crystallin? Never! Alexandra White would be so jealous.*

Celeste dropped off Stella and Zenda. The others had not returned home yet. When they reached Stella's bedroom, Zenda saw herself in the mirror.

A new person stared back at her. Zenda barely recognized herself.

"You look fabulous, Zen," Stella said, hugging her. "You are so much more fun than Kaitlyn. I wish you were my sister instead."

A muffled sob came from the doorway. Zenda turned to see Kaitlyn standing there. She turned and ran away.

"Kaitlyn!" Zenda cried.

The Cavern
of Kelara

Stella grabbed Zenda's arm.

"Let her go," she said. "She's so immature."

Zenda held back. But she didn't feel good about it.

"Kaitlyn's nice," she said. "Even if she is only ten." She wanted Stella to understand that one of her favorite things about her cousins was how different they were.

Stella frowned. "She may be nice, but she's no fun at all."

Aunt Nina poked her head into the room. "How are you feeling, Zenda?" she asked, then she stopped and gave Zenda a surprised look. "My, you look nice. Where did you get that dress?"

"I'm feeling much better," Zenda said, not sure how to answer the second question.

"Celeste came by and loaned it to her," Stella said, turning and giving Zenda a grin. "Wasn't that nice of her?"

"It certainly was," Aunt Nina said. "I

just came to tell you that we're having supper soon. I hope you feel like eating, Zenda."

"Of course!" Zenda said, realizing the others must have eaten lunch in Thalissa, while Zenda and Stella were out shopping.

Zenda's parents were just as surprised as Aunt Nina to see the change in Zenda.

"You look different, starshine," Vetiver said. "Just like a Crystallite. I hope you won't move here one day like my little brother did."

"Vetiver!" Verbena cried, horrified at the thought.

The thought intrigued Zenda. There was no rule that said she had to stay on Azureblue once she got older. She could move anywhere she wanted to . . . even Crystallin.

The rest of the night, Zenda thought thankfully, was fairly quiet. Uncle Ciro brought out a board with strange markings on it, and a jar of colored stones. He taught Zenda and her parents how to play *vinku*, a traditional Crystallin game.

Everyone played but Stella. She lounged on one of the white couches and watched. When the game was over, she walked up to Aunt Nina.

"I want to take Zenda on a picnic tomorrow, with Trisha and Celeste," she said. "Is that okay?"

Zenda studied her cousin's face. Did Stella really have a picnic planned . . . or something else in mind?

"That sounds lovely," Aunt Nina said. "I'm assuming Kaitlyn is invited too?"

Across the room, Zenda saw Kaitlyn's face light up.

"Kaitlyn?" Stella protested. "But she's too young."

Aunt Nina shook her head. "Ten years old is not too young for a picnic, Stella. Kaitlyn deserves to spend time with Zenda just as much as you do. I will not discuss this any further."

Stella sighed. "Fine," she said.

Of course, as they got ready for bed later, Stella made it clear that having Kaitlyn along was not fine.

"But we'll have fun anyway, Zen," Stella said. "I promise."

Zenda was putting her blue dress in her bag when she remembered something — Persuaja's letter. She dug through the clothes there until she found it. She opened the letter and found a small note written in purple ink, in Persuaja's curly handwriting. She read the note under the light of a glowing rock.

Zenda,

Your journey is taking you to strange and new places, isn't it? I wanted you to know that although I may not be there to assist you, my thoughts will be with you. And I must ask you to remember one thing, Zenda: remember who you are.

Until we meet again,
Persuaja

Zenda stared at the note. It was nice to know that Persuaja was thinking of her, but Zenda knew that the note had to mean something more than that. *Remember who you are.* The words sounded cryptic, but they were simple, weren't they? How could someone *forget* who they were? It didn't make sense. Puzzled, Zenda drifted off to sleep.

The girls set off for the picnic late the next morning. Uncle Ciro had packed them a basket of peanut butter and honey sandwiches and jugs of orange-flavored water. Stella handed the basket to Kaitlyn.

"Here you go," she said. "If you're coming, you might as well be useful."

Kaitlyn scowled at her sister, but didn't complain out loud. The girls set off down the road and found Trisha and Celeste waiting for them a few blocks away.

"Sorry," Stella said apologetically. "Nina said I had to bring her."

Everyone knew that "her" meant

Kaitlyn. Trisha shrugged. "Just as long as she doesn't keep us from—"

"She won't," Stella said quickly. "It'll be fine."

Keep us from what? Zenda wondered, and got that nervous feeling again. Were they really going on a picnic—or did Stella have something else in mind?

But when they reached the picnic site, Zenda wondered if she had worried for nothing. They hiked up the hills to the top of a cliff. A beautiful stream ran alongside them. Celeste spread a blanket on the ground, and Stella took the picnic basket from Kaitlyn.

They ate the sandwiches and spent some time talking under the bright blue Crystallin sky. Stella told Zenda what her school was like, and Trisha and Celeste ran off a list of the cutest boys in the village. Zenda was enjoying herself so much that she didn't realize that Kaitlyn had wandered off. She was kneeling by the bank of the stream.

"I'll be right back," Zenda told the others, and went to join Kaitlyn.

Her cousin was staring at a clump of plants growing out of the water. Zenda recognized them—they looked just like the water lavender back home.

"We don't have too many wild plants here," Kaitlyn said. "It's nice to come visit once in a while."

"You visit the plants?" Zenda asked. It seemed like a curious thing to do.

Kaitlyn shrugged. "I like to watch them change and grow," she said. "Once, these gold-colored bugs nested in the plant and started eating all the leaves."

"Xander bugs," Zenda said. "We have those on Azureblue, too."

Kaitlyn nodded. "I thought I would lose the water lavender forever. So I tried to find a way to get rid of the bugs."

Zenda smiled. Kaitlyn sounded just like

Mykal now. "What did you do?" Zenda asked.

"I noticed the bugs stayed away from the thorn leaf," Kaitlyn said, pointing to a scrubby-looking plant growing from a nearby rock. "So I boiled the leaves in water and made an infusion. I sprayed it on the water lavender, and it kept the bugs away."

Zenda was impressed. "You have to come visit Azureblue sometime, Kaitlyn," she said. "You would love it there!"

"I know," Kaitlyn said, sighing. "Sometimes I look up at the sky and see Azureblue at night. I always make a wish that I can go there someday."

Zenda felt a presence behind her, and turned to see Stella, Trisha, and Celeste there.

"Is it time to go?" Zenda asked.

"Not exactly," Stella said. "We want to see something before we go. The Cavern of Kelara."

"Kelara!" Kaitlyn sounded shocked.

"Are you out of your mind, Stella?"

Trisha sighed. "I knew she would be a problem."

"Just listen," Stella said. "The entrance is close by. Some friends of mine were there last week. They said it's not dangerous at all."

"Dangerous?" Zenda asked.

"The Cavern of Kelara used to be mined for memory stones years ago," Kaitlyn said. "But it got too dangerous. Too many cave-ins. It's been off-limits for ages. That's why memory stones are so rare these days."

"The elders around here think everything's too dangerous," Trisha sneered.

Celeste shrugged. "It can't hurt to check it out. So are we going?"

"No way!" Kaitlyn said, rising to her feet. "That's the stupidest thing I've ever heard. I'm going home."

Kaitlyn stomped off. Trisha gave Stella a look of alarm.

"She won't tell," Stella said. "She never does. Let's just go."

The other girls started to walk away, but Zenda hesitated. If what Kaitlyn said was true, then going into the cavern really was a stupid idea.

"What's the matter, Zen?" Stella asked. "Kait's little story didn't scare you, did it?"

Zenda's Vision

"No, it didn't scare me," Zenda said. "It just made sense. I think Kaitlyn's right. I'm not going."

Stella shrugged. "Fine with me. I thought you were more mature than that, I guess."

Stella and her friends turned and walked away, giggling. Zenda felt her cheeks grow hot. She saw Kaitlyn in the distance, and ran after her.

"Kaitlyn, stop!" Zenda called.

Her cousin looked puzzled. "You're coming with me?" she asked.

"Yes," Zenda replied. "I got into big trouble on Azureblue a few weeks ago for going someplace I shouldn't have gone. I'm not going to do it again."

Kaitlyn smiled, and Zenda had a sudden thought. *Remember who you are.* Is that what Persuaja had meant? Sneaking in to see her gazing ball wasn't a very smart thing to do, but at least she had learned something from it—and remembered it.

Zenda looked over her shoulder. "I hope they'll be okay," she said.

"They always are," Kaitlyn said with a resigned tone to her voice. "Everything always works out for Stella."

When they got back to the house, they found a note on the kitchen table. Kaitlyn picked it up and read it. "They've gone back into Thalissa to do some shopping," she said. "Sorry. I guess you're stuck with me."

"I'm not stuck at all!" Zenda said, feeling sorry for Kaitlyn. "What would you like to do?"

Kaitlyn thought. "Could I see Luna again?" she asked.

"Sure," Zenda said.

Zenda retrieved Luna from Stella's bedroom and brought her back upstairs. It was too bright and sunny out to be underground. She and Kaitlyn sat cross-legged next to the bathing pool and talked. The waterfall sounded like soft music in the background.

"She's so soft," Kaitlyn said, stroking Luna's colorful yarn hair. "Everything on Crystallin is hard. Hard as rocks. I bet it's not like that on Azureblue."

"No, it's not," Zenda said, and for a moment her thoughts drifted to all of the soft things back home—Oscar's brown fur; fields of new grass; fields of dandelions and their white, puffy seeds. For a second, she was horribly homesick.

"You know," she said. "Yesterday, when you said you look up at Azureblue in the sky and wish you could go there? Well, I used to do that with Crystallin. To me, it seemed like it would be the most wonderful place."

"Do you still think so?" Kaitlyn asked.

"I do," Zenda said. "But I think Azureblue is pretty wonderful, too."

Kaitlyn silently thought about this. She handed Luna back to Zenda.

"Thanks for showing me Luna again," she said. "Do you want to go to the greenhouse with me? It's time to feed the plants."

"All right," Zenda replied. "I'll just put Luna back first."

Zenda looked into Luna's smiling face—and then froze.

A strange feeling crept over her. It happened sometimes when she talked to Luna. She felt suddenly light-headed, and a mist clouded her vision.

Zenda saw her grandmother's face, her bright blue eyes in a face framed by snow-white hair. Delphina looked worried.

Then the image of Delphina's face faded, and another image appeared. It was a cavern. Stella, Trisha, and Celeste were huddled in a corner. Several feet in front of them loomed a large, yellow snake with red stripes across its back. The snake looked ready to strike.

Zenda gasped and dropped the doll.

"What happened, Zenda?" Kaitlyn

asked. "You got this weird look in your eyes."

Zenda found her breath. "I can't explain it," she said. "But I saw something. Stella and her friends, in the cavern. And there was a snake."

Kaitlyn looked fearful. "A yellow snake with red stripes?"

Zenda nodded.

"This is bad," Kaitlyn said. "That's a yellow *yowi* snake. They're deadly poisonous. They live all over the caverns."

"We've got to get help!" Zenda said.

"No time," Kaitlyn said. "Unless maybe—" She took off running.

Zenda followed her to the greenhouse. Kaitlyn raced to a shelf in the back, where a plant with spiky green leaves and a large, red flower was growing. Zenda had never seen one on Azureblue.

"One of the few wild plants on Crystallin," Kaitlyn said. "I read about it in school. The plant's nectar is poisonous to the *yowi*. They won't go near it. I started growing them to see if I could make a snake repellent, but I haven't figured out how to get the nectar out yet."

Zenda had a thought. "Bring it," she said. "I think I know what to do."

Facing
the Yowi

Zenda and Kaitlyn raced back to the picnic site. Kaitlyn knew where the entrance to the cavern was. It had been blocked by rocks years ago, but determined teens like Stella, who had the gift of levitation, had managed to move some of the rocks aside over time, inch by inch, until there was enough room to pass through.

The cousins slipped into the entrance. Kaitlyn had grabbed two of the glowing stones as they left the house, and handed one to Zenda.

"We have to go quietly," Kaitlyn whispered. "The snake will strike if it hears a sudden noise."

Zenda nodded. The two crept down the dark pathway. As they walked, Zenda thought about what would happen once they found the snake.

On the way to the caverns, Kaitlyn had told Zenda more about the plant, which she called a *turga* flower. In the wild, the plants would release a spray of nectar whenever a predator got near. The nectar had evolved as a kind of defense mechanism.

So far, Kaitlyn hadn't been able to get it to release the spray. From what she had learned, the stored nectar itself didn't have the power to repel anything. Something changed it chemically as it traveled through the flower and was sprayed out.

Zenda had been thinking about this. The *turga* flower might release its spray when it got close to the snake—but that would be dangerous to whoever was holding the flower. She had to convince the flower to release its spray some other way.

She'd have to use her *kani*. She just hoped it would work.

After a few minutes, they heard a soft, whimpering sound. They slowed their steps, and soon saw Stella, Trisha, and Celeste huddled against one of the cavern walls. In front of them, with its back to Zenda and Kaitlyn, was the *yowi*.

Stella's eyes widened when she saw them, and Trisha almost said something, but Celeste clasped her hand in front of her mouth. The *yowi* swayed back and forth on its tail, as though it was savoring the picture of the three terrified girls. Zenda couldn't see its face, but it wasn't difficult to picture the snake's sharp fangs. She shuddered.

But she had to do something. She took the *turga* plant from Kaitlyn and placed her hand on the stem. Then she closed her eyes.

Please, Zenda asked silently. *Release your spray. Send the snake away. Help us.*

But Zenda only got a feeling of peace in return from the plant. Peace, and a quiet calm.

It doesn't sense the snake, Zenda realized. *It's too far away.*

Zenda tried again. *Snake*, she told the plant. *Big, yellow snake.*

Again, Zenda got nothing. She opened her eyes. The *yowi* had inched closer to the girls now. Stella and her friends were holding their breath.

Then it hit Zenda. Fear. The plant needed to feel fear. She could do that.

Zenda closed her eyes again. This time, she sent feelings of fear to the *turga*. Fear that the snake would harm her cousin. She imagined being Stella, facing the terrible *yowi*, its thin reptile eyes fixed on her . . .

Then came a sudden hissing sound, but it was not coming from the *yowi*. The *turga* plant had let loose a cloud of red liquid. The droplets sizzled when they hit the cave floor.

The *yowi* turned its head, and for a horrifying second Zenda saw its eyes focused on her. Then it lowered its body to the ground and crawled away down the path, away from the girls—and the *turga* flower.

"Hurry!" Kaitlyn cried.

She didn't have to. Stella and her friends charged from the corner, nearly knocking them down. They were all safely aboveground a few seconds later.

One More
Surprise

"Thank you, thank you, Zenda," Stella said, throwing her arms around her cousin. "You saved us from being snake meat."

"I just helped," Zenda said, stepping back. "It was all Kaitlyn's idea. She was the one who knew about the *turga* flower. You probably would be snake meat if it wasn't for her."

"Kait?" Stella asked, surprised. But she then she grabbed her sister in a huge hug. "You are amazing! I will never make fun of your greenhouse again."

Trisha and Celeste each hugged Kaitlyn, who broke into a shy smile.

"Let's go to Ruby's," Celeste suggested. "My treat."

"Even me?" Kaitlyn asked.

"Of course you, silly," Stella said, shaking her head. "You can be so immature sometimes."

The girls drank lemonade at the cafe. Zenda listened as Stella told the story of how

113

they had come across the *yowi* in the cavern.

"It's a good thing we saw it before it saw us," Stella said.

"And it's really good that you two showed up when you did," Trisha said. "Why did you come back to the cavern, anyway?"

Zenda and Kaitlyn looked at each other. Zenda smiled.

"I guess that'll have to be our secret," she said. "If that's okay."

"Well, since you saved our lives, you can have a little secret if you want," Stella said, teasing.

That night, the whole family went to a restaurant in Thalissa. Zenda wore the green dress she had brought from home. It was fun feeling like a Crystallite for a while, but after all the excitement today, she wanted to feel like Zenda again.

Riding home on the zephyr, Zenda found herself looking up at the night sky. Stars twinkled overhead. Kaitlyn tapped her on the arm and pointed to a pale blue star just over the hills.

"That's Azureblue," Kaitlyn said.

Hearing Kaitlyn say the name of her planet made Zenda feel like she was hearing it for the first time. It sounded so beautiful. Azureblue. And tomorrow she would be back there again. Zenda smiled.

Back at the house, the cousins spent their last night together talking in Stella's room. As the night got light, Stella began braiding her sister's hair. Zenda decided to write in her journal.

⎯⎯⎯⎯⎯⎯

I have only been on Crystallin a few days, but it seems like ages! So much has happened. I will never forget those snakes eyes when it looked at me. So creepy . . .

I feel like I've changed a little bit,

too. When I first came here, I didn't even want to talk to Kaitlyn about plants. I wanted to be with Stella, who seemed so much more exciting and older. But I think I had a better time with Kaitlyn in her greenhouse than I did at that party in the cavern. And the way Kaitlyn figured out how to use the turga plant . . . well, that was pretty exciting to me! I can't wait to tell Mykal about it.

I'm sad to be leaving Crystallin, but it will be good to be home again. I miss Camille. And Oscar. And Mykal. And Persuaja. And maybe even plants!

Cosmically yours,
Zenda

116

Zenda had barely closed the journal when she heard a familiar sound, like the chiming of tiny bells. A white mist appeared in the air in front of her.

Zenda opened her palm, and watched a tiny crystal shard appear. Kaitlyn and Stella crowded around her.

"What just happened?" Kaitlyn asked.

"It's one of the missing pieces of my gazing ball," Zenda said, staring at the shard in wonder. "It's got a musing on it."

Zenda looked at the tiny writing, which read, *Mirrors reflect but people shine.*

"That's wonderful!" Kaitlyn said.

Stella thoughtfully looked at the crystal shard. "I used to think musings were useless," she said slowly. "But you know, I think this one makes good sense."

Zenda smiled at her cousins, who smiled back at her. Right now, they both looked like the most beautiful people in the universe.

"That's my fourth musing," Zenda said,

slipping the piece of gazing ball into the pouch she wore around her neck. "Nine more to go."

"You'll get them all, Zen," Stella said, giving her a hug. "I know you will."

Farewell to Crystallin

The next morning, everyone woke up early—even Stella. Zenda and her parents were scheduled to be at the transport tunnels later that afternoon, and they all wanted to make the most of the time they had left.

"Is there anything special you would like to do today, Zenda?" Aunt Nina asked at breakfast.

Zenda thought. "Well, I would like to get some presents for my friends back home," she said. "Mykal and Camille have never been off Azureblue before."

"What kind of things do they like?" Stella asked.

"Mykal loves plants," Zenda replied. "And Camille—well, she loves bugs, mostly. But I'm sure she'd like anything sparkly or shiny, too."

Kaitlyn shyly looked up from her plate of ambrosia. "I could give you some *turga* seeds for Mykal. If you think he'd like them."

"He'd love them!" Zenda said. "That's a great idea."

"I know where we can go to find something for Camille," Stella said. "There's a little shop right here in the village."

"May I come too?"

At first, Zenda thought Kaitlyn had asked the question, but it was her own mother. She looked at Verbena's eager face; even though her hair was streaked with gray, she sometimes looked like a teenager herself.

"We'll all go," Aunt Nina said.

So they spent the morning in the little shop, which to Zenda seemed just as fascinating as the Palace of Gems. Every shelf in the shop held bins of shimmering stones and delicate jewelry. Zenda found a pin for Camille that looked like a dragonfly, with bright green gems embedded in its body and wings. A polished, purple piece of amethyst reminded her of Persuaja, so she bought that, too.

121

Zenda was looking for a souvenir for herself when Stella and Kaitlyn approached her. Kaitlyn held out her hand. A small box rested in her palm.

"It's for you, Zenda," she said. "From both of us."

Zenda opened the box to see a light blue crystal carved into the shape of a flower. It hung from a white silk cord.

"It's a crystal, to remind you of me," Stella said.

"And a flower, to remind you of *me*," Kaitlyn added.

Zenda thought it was beautiful. As she put it around her neck, she realized the necklace reminded her of two other things, too: Crystallin and Azureblue. A world of gems, and a world of plants. She was also pleased to see in the box a pair of butterfly slippers just for her!

"Thank you so much," Zenda said. "I will never forget either of you!"

Back at the house, Zenda remembered that Verbena had suggested she pack some of the products from the karmacy for her cousins. She gave Stella a bottle of Butterfly Wings body lotion, and a bottle of Rolling Meadow bubble bath seemed just perfect for Kaitlyn.

And then it was time to go. Zenda felt as though she had barely arrived on Crystallin. The days had passed so quickly.

Uncle Ciro took them all to the transport building. Zenda and her parents got in line. Uncle Ciro gave each one of them a big bear hug.

"Take care of my big brother," he said, his blue eyes twinkling. "Make sure he doesn't forget us."

"I will," Zenda said, her eyes suddenly filling with tears. Why did her uncle and his family have to live so far away?

"Don't worry, Zenda," he said. "We'll come by for a visit soon. We could all use a helping of nice fresh vegetables."

That made Zenda feel better, for a second. Then her mother called to her.

"It's our turn, Zenda," she said.

Zenda waved good-bye to her cousins one last time. Then she followed her parents into the transport building.

It was time to go home.

A Moonlight
Musing

Zenda blinked as the door of the transport tunnel opened up. The trip back to Azureblue had been just as strange as the trip to Crystallin, but at least she knew what to expect this time.

Verbena had gone ahead of her. She gave Zenda a hug and led her outside.

"It's good to be home, isn't it?" she said. Then she took a deep breath. "I can smell the green in the air. I missed that smell."

Zenda sniffed the air, too, and she knew what her mother meant. It sounded strange, that something could smell like a color, but that was how the air on Azureblue smelled: green. There was no other word to describe it, really.

Vetiver emerged from the transport building just as Niko pulled up with the cart. Zenda climbed up, settled back, and took in the sights around her as the cart clattered down the path. Tall trees rose up on either side — soft green pines; tall, sturdy oaks; maple trees with their delicate branches; and many others. The sun was sinking into the horizon, streaking the sky with shades of red and purple. Birds flew from tree to tree, settling in for a night's rest.

It's just as beautiful as Crystallin, Zenda thought. *Just in a different way.*

In the front of the cart, Vetiver and Niko were talking about what had happened at the karmacy while they were away.

"We could use some more water lavender," Niko was saying. "There have been extra orders for the tonic, and the plants will stop blooming soon, won't they?"

Vetiver turned around and gave Zenda a pleading look. "I know we've just got back, but — "

"I don't mind," Zenda said, interrupting him. And honestly, she didn't. It would be nice to be around plants again.

Soon, the wagon climbed up the path to Zenda's house. To her surprise, she saw two figures sitting on rocking chairs on the front porch. As she got closer, she saw a boy with shaggy blond hair and a girl with nut brown skin and curly, dark hair. Mykal and Camille!

Oscar jumped off Mykal's lap and ran to Zenda as she climbed up the stairs. She picked him up, and he licked her cheeks. Zenda laughed and put him down.

"It's so good to see you!" she told her friends.

"We missed you, Zenda," Camille said.

"You've got to tell us what it was like on Crystallin," Mykal said. "Were there any plants there?"

"And there's a spring party tonight in the village square," Camille added. "Do you want to go?"

Zenda didn't know which question to answer first. Her mother came to her rescue.

"Zenda needs to get grounded after her trip in the transport tunnels," Verbena said. "Let's see if we can't get something to eat first, all right?"

They ate some bread and cheese on the porch, and Zenda felt more like herself again. She didn't much feel like going to the party, though.

"I promised my dad I'd harvest some water lavender," she said. "After everything that happened on Crystallin, I think that's where I'd rather be tonight."

"Then we'll help you," Mykal said.

"Sure," Camille added, smiling.

Zenda smiled back. She could travel all over the universe, and still not find friends like Mykal and Camille.

They made their way to the pond just as darkness was setting. Camille rowed the boat while Mykal and Zenda harvested the plants.

Zenda was eager for news. "Did anything interesting happen while we were gone?" she asked.

"Well, Marion Rose mailed out an announcement about the school trip this year," Camille said. "You won't believe where we're going—Aquaria!"

"That's right," Mykal said. "So soon, you won't be the only one who's traveled off Azureblue."

Zenda let the news sink in. Aquaria was one of Azureblue's four moons. She had just gotten her feet back on Azureblue, and she'd be leaving again soon! She wasn't sure how she felt about that.

"Now you have to tell us all about Crystallin," Camille said eagerly.

So Zenda launched into the story. She told them about the party in the cavern, the trip to the Palace of Gems, the picnic on the cliff, and how she and Kaitlyn had saved Stella and the others in the Cavern of Kelara.

Camille shuddered. "It's a good thing you didn't go into the cavern with Stella and her friends," she said thoughtfully. "You probably would have all got bitten by that *yowi*!"

"I know," Zenda said. "I'm glad I made the right decision. You know, Persuaja wrote me a note and told me to remember who I am. I guess that's what I did. And it helped. It even helped me figure out how to use the *turga* plant."

Mykal grinned in the silly way he had. "So who are you, Zenda?"

It wasn't an easy question to answer. But Zenda decided to try. "I'm Zenda. From Azureblue. I have *kani*, even though sometimes it makes me crazy to work with plants all the time. I even thought I'd be happier on Crystallin, with no plants around. But you know what? I missed them. Plants are a part of who I am."

The air in front of them began to glimmer. At first, Zenda thought it was moonlight reflecting off the water. But then she

131

heard the sound of bells.

"Another one?" Zenda asked breathlessly.

A green crystal shard appeared in the air and fell gently onto Zenda's lap.

"Zenda, is that a musing?" Camille asked, her voice full of wonder. "You told me what happened, but I didn't think it would be like this!"

Mykal looked transfixed, like he couldn't quite believe what had happened.

"It's a piece of my missing gazing ball," Zenda explained. "There's a musing etched into it."

Zenda read the musing aloud.

"Be true to who you are."

Then she grinned. Persuaja's note had been a kind of clue, leading her in the right direction.

"This is one musing I will have to remember," Zenda said.

Later that night, Zenda tried to stay awake long enough to write in her journal.

I can't believe I got my bibth musing! And I am so glad it happened in bront ob Camille and Mykal, too. It makes everything seem more real, somehow.

The trip to Crystallin ended up being the best vacation ever, but not bor the reasons I thought it would be. The planet is beautibul, but I could have met my cousins on a planet made ob mud and dirt and I still would have had a wonderbul time. I miss Stella and Kaitlyn already. I hope they come to visit soon!

I have the crystal blower to remember them by. And I have the musing I got there, too. Can you believe I bound a musing on another planet?

I guess that's good, since we're going to Aquaria soon. The thought of going to Aquaria makes me a little nervous, actually. I've heard it's pretty wild up there—raging rivers, towering waterfalls, and strange creatures that no one has been able to capture or study. What kind of school trip is that going to be?

I guess I will find out soon! And who knows . . . maybe I will find another piece of my gazing ball while I'm there. A girl can dream, can't she?

Cosmically yours,
Zenda